Babystar

Story and Picture
by
Annie Helm

This is a story
for all the Babystars
on the Earth
and the Angels
who love them.

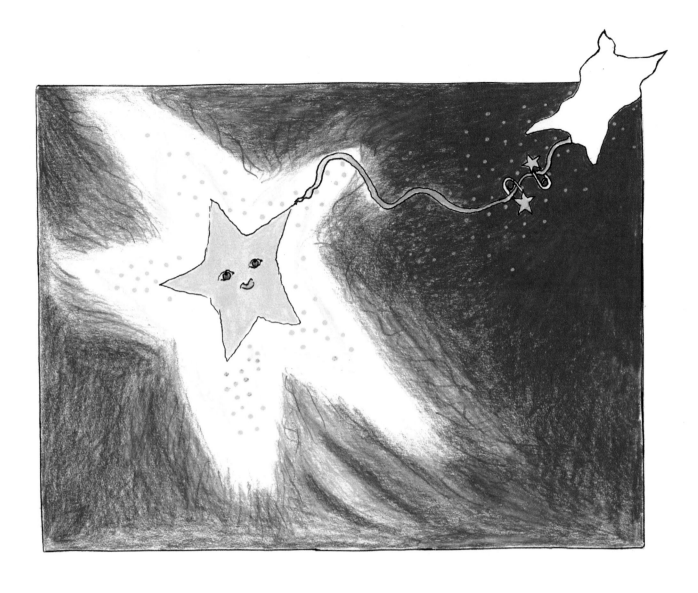

Once upon a night
Babystar was born
to the sky.

Babystar was so happy to be part of the
big blue sky as she twinkled with love
for her new world around her.

She sent special sparkles of love
to old Mr. Moon and smiled
as Mrs. Sun began a new day.

A new day was dawning...
morning had come.

Tired now, Babystar folded
her points inwardly and
flickered to sleep...
happy to be one night old.

Suddenly, the little star was
awakened by a very loud
MOO...OOO.
The Moo spoke,
"I am the cow that jumps
over the moo...oon.
Mr. Moo...oon is very upset
and wants to see you right away.
Come with me!"

And so she did...

Babystar jumped on Cow's back
and away they flew toward
the night and Mr. Moon.

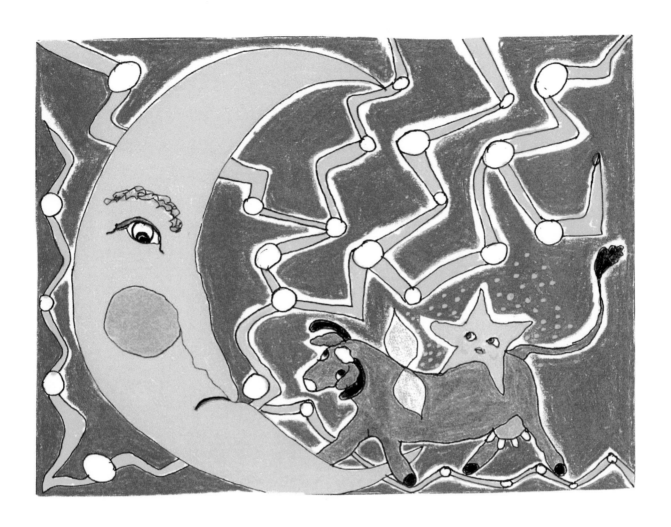

Old Mr. Moon was in a wobble
and began to mutter when they landed

KERPLOP

on top of his trouble. "Look what
you've do...do...done Babystar with
all those silly sparkles you sent me
last night! You've zig-zagged my
moonbeams and put holes in
my light." He was not pleased!

Babystar jumped on top of Mr. Moon's head and
tried to give him a big twinkle from her heart
to make him feel better but it didn't work.
Old Mr. Moon went into a grumble
and began to mumble.
"You've messed up my mo...mo...moonbeams
and now jump on my head!?
What is the ma...ma...matter with you?
Don't you kno...kno...know this silly twinkling
that you do from the heart is so
sta...sta...star-struck and POINTLESS!" *

*Pointless means without points and unnecessary.
It's the worst word you could ever say to a Babystar!

Babystar looked down at her points
and became confused. She didn't
know how to twinkle any other way
except from her heart! The little star
began to do the worst thing a
Babystar can do. She cried big black
tears of sadness all over herself
putting the light out in one of her
beautiful points!

Babystar sadly watched as her light
disappeared into the darkness.

Cow and Mr. Moon looked on.
Old Mr. Moon was very sorry for what
he said and wished he could take his
pointless words back. But it was too late!
The damage had been done!
Babystar was pointless!

She needed help!

A little pink cloud was drifting by
and let Babystar rest
upon her billows.

"We'll go and see Mrs. Sun.
She'll help you shine again... you'll see!"
the little cloud said.

Babystar had found a friend.

But Mrs. Sun had no time for Babystar to-day.
She was too busy taking care of
the Earth and making things grow.

"Come back on a rainy day
when I am less busy,"
she said.

"We'll bake cookies and
have sun-tea together.
Now run along dear."

But Babystar did not know where to run to.
She began to worry about her twinkles
which is the worst thing a baby star can do.
The worry became so big, it began to creep
over her body like a big black snake...
squeezing out the light in her second point.
The little star was in big trouble!
What was she to do!

"Do not worry, Babystar,"
the little cloud said.
"We'll go and see Mr. Storm.
He has lots of power and energy.
He'll make you twinkle again, you'll see."

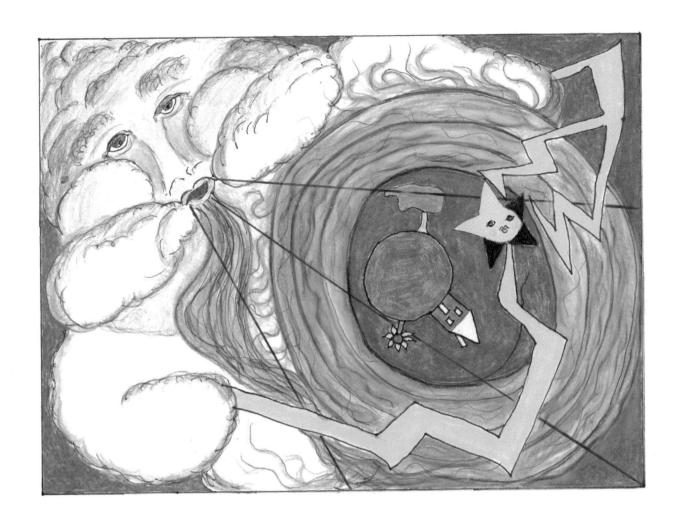

Mr. Storm was more than happy to help out.
He whooshed* Babystar around the Earth
five times and bolted her with lightning.
He bellowed and blew,
"Twinkle, Babystar, twinkle!"

*Whooshed is Babystar's favorite word for moving.

But the storm did not work. It just gave
Babystar a bad tummy-ache and a dizzy
feeling in her points, which is the worst
thing a baby star can feel.

OUCH!

she said, as she watched her
third point flicker and fade.
Poor little Babystar!

What was she to do!

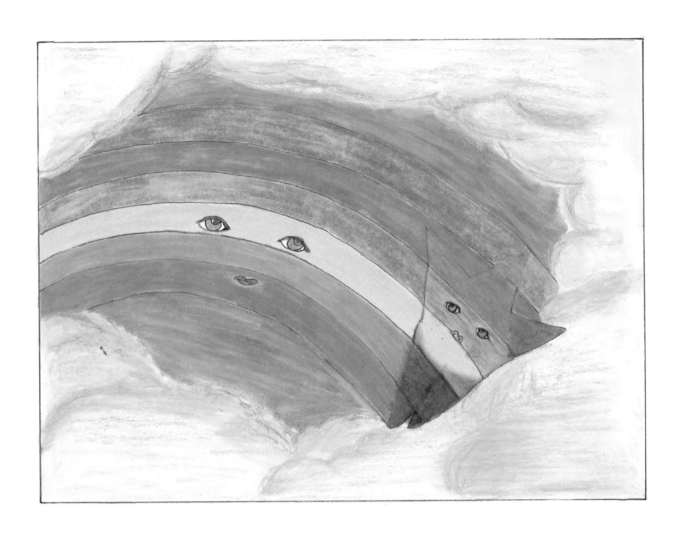

After the storm, Rainbow appeared
peeking out of the clouds.
"I will help you glow again,"
she softly said, as she shimmered
her colors of light upon Babystar.

Lovingly, Rainbow stretched down to Earth
as a giant bridge for Babystar to slide on.
"Jump on my colored slide to Earth.
Bathe in my magical pot of gold.
That will make you shine again!"
she said.

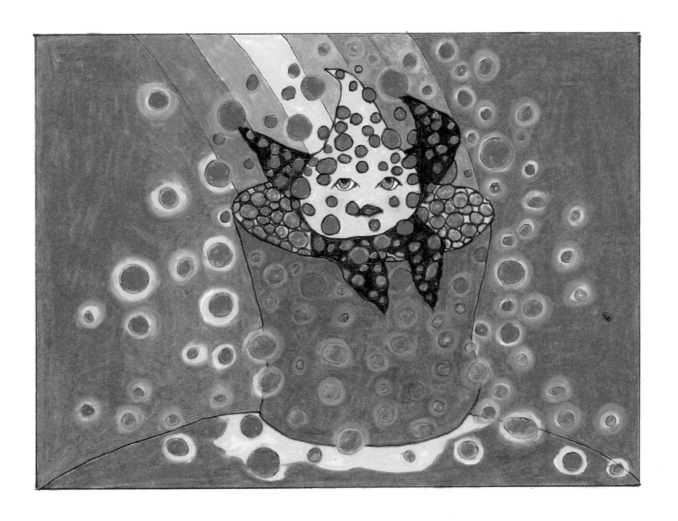

But alas, the gold was not magical
for Babystar. It just went

CLINK-CLANK

and felt cold as it fell upon her points.
The little star began to shiver and feel homesick,
which is the worst thing a Babystar can feel.
"Oh no" cried Babystar,
as she watched her fourth point go out!
Babystar had only one point of light left.
What was she to do?

j

Rain came out and heard Babystar's cry
and came to her rescue.
"I'll wash your darkness away,"
she gently said,
as she poured her crystal drops of light into
a shower for the little star. But the raindrops
were too heavy on Babystar's body
and swamped out her very last point of light.
All her points were gone now!

There was nothing left of Babystar...
just a little ball of golden light.

That's all she was!

Her rosy cheeks and twinkles were all
gone! Babystar fell into a
deep and dark sleep....

Suddenly, a beautiful angel of light
appeared through a golden mist...
Babystar thought she was dreaming.

The angel flew Babystar up to the
most magical place in the sky.

There before her eyes...tucked away
in the clouds was an angel house with
a garden of flowers growing hearts.

Babystar thought she was in heaven...
there was so much love
and magic around her.

They sat and dined on star-cookies
and milky-way shakes
inside the angel's house.

After supper the angel took Babystar out into
her garden of love. There she wrapped her
large wings around Babystar and gently said,
"I am here to help you twinkle again."

"How?"
asked Babystar.

"By knowing the
'angel secret'"
she said.

The 'angel secret'

"What is it? What is it?"
Babystar asked excitedly, as they
sat down under the heart tree.

The angel reached up and touched
Babystar's heart, ever so softly,
as she whispered the
'angel secret'
to her.

You never really lost your light
Babystar!
The light is inside of you!

Babystar began to smile
the biggest smile she has ever smiled,
which is the best thing a Babystar can do!
She could not believe her points!
She was tingling all over with love!

And then the most

wonderful of wonderfuls
happened...

Babystar
was
twinkling
again!

The angel and Babystar
jumped up and down with joy!

Babystar gave the angel the biggest hug and thanked her for the 'angel secret' of light. The angel kissed each one of Babystar's points and said,

"Now you will never be pointless again." "I love you dear angel and I will never forget you," said Babystar.

"And I love you. I will always be watching over you...for you are my little star of light shining bright for me."

Twilight had come...
the night was near.

The angel held Babystar in her arms
as she looked down upon the Earth
with a knowing smile and said,

"And now it is time for you to shine
your light upon the world little star."

And with a twinkling of love,
Babystar was back in the sky
where she belonged.
Wishing everyone...

a very good night and...

the sweetest of dreams...

to be continued...